On Reflection

Dedication:

This book is dedicated to both my sons, Niall and Blaine,
who made being a mother the loveliest of experiences.
The shared hugs, love and mutual support,
together with the open-mindedness and humour
are part of what has made me so proud.
With my love to you both always.

About This Book:

Welcome to my first book of poetry

My life, like the lives of most people, if not everyone,
is full to the brim with randomness.
The moments of regret, the moments to treasure.
People I meet or would like to meet.
Days that go to plan, and those that don't!
Ambitions unaccomplished and all the experiences I've had...

In a nutshell my writing has been like the flip of a coin,
and a shuffle of a pack of cards.
Whatever comes my way, I write about.
And this has shaped who I am for the last six months or so
My final poem of the book, named 'Got To Love An Umbrella'
Is part of an idea for another poem which will be included in my
second book by the name of 'Sunhats And Raincoats'

Wherever you are,
I just want to give you the following message –
I am grateful that you have got my book in your hands and hope
that you can find at least some of my poetry relatable or simply
enjoyable!

Thank you

Alys

Table Of Contents:

For The Senses ... Pages 15 - 25
The friend -17
What Light Can Do -18
The Painted Smile -19
Some Kind Of Energy -20
Mesmerising -21
As It Rotates -22
The Chiming -23
There Was Space (part one) -24
There Was Space (part two) -25

Lighter Notes Pages 27 - 33
Stories People Tell -28
Happy Times -29
Hand Written -30
Are You Alright Love? -31
Free -32
To Be A Cat -33

For The Diary ... Pages 35 - 45
Some Things -36
Go Adrift -37
The Three Minute Timer -38
The Downpour -39
Saint Agnes - 40
Really, Always - 41
But All I Am - 42
And So It Was - 43
The Sail Away - 44
The Fading Light -45

The Hidden Meanings ... Pages 47 - 57

Was I Ever Born? - 48

The Fern - 49

Of The Time -50

In The Garden -51

The Maiden At Sea -52

The Red Kite -53

Distant Miles -54

What We Borrow -55

It Didn't Exist -56

In The Red -57

Just Round The Corner ... pages 59 - 69

The Other Day - 60

Under The Pier - 61

We No Longer Roam -62

Cupid's Arrow - 63

The Unsung Dance - 64

Sto Bene - 65

Dead Of The Night - 66

Broken Fences - 67

This Heart Of Mine - 68

Living In Hope - 69

For The Soul ... Pages 71 - 81

Hummingbirds -72

Letting It Happen -73

No Tomorrow -74

Shadow Angle (part one) -75

Shadow Angle (part two) -76

The Definition -77 & 78

On The Mural -79

A Fine Glance - 80

Thoughts Out - 81 [pto]

Deeper Notes ... Pages 83 - 89
Modernity - 84
Anatomical - 85
Merging - 86
The Final One - 87
The Blue Room - 88
It's Getting Late - 89

Hand In Hand ... Pages 91 - 97
The Quiet - 92
The Tumbledown - 93
The Escape - 94
There In Our Minds - 95
Got To Love An Umbrella - 96

For The senses

The Friend

You twist as you turn
You bend, and stretch
On grass and soil, you lie, and rest
What you always do, and without any flaw,

Is shout 'peek a boo' and play 'tug of war'

And as for us...we 'hide and seek,'
We skeletal climb, as branches creak

And as we talk, your bow will bend
You sway with skill, my dancing friend!

With this, you show us, clustered stars
Above you'll be, the tower you are
Lived upon, for those that crawl,
You nourish wisely...
so pure the fall
You embrace this rain, but later on,
you'll kiss the sun, til sunlight gone

You chatter...like laughter
You filter the light,
like a lamp being held in the midst of the night
From chatter, to rattle, your leaves touch the bark
And they crumble with ambient sounds in the dark

What Light Can Do

One light, one beam
One skyscraper of a dream
One dazzle of a ship, in the distant metal sea
One jewel on your wrist,
One thousand little twists
One light, one lonely beam,
Within this mystery

One gem, one solar light,
That sneak up on the night
That simply keep us occupied
One ship now out of sight
One pattern urging others, to spin across the wall
One moment of reflection...
Before we touch them all

Two circles come together,
Two jewels, set in place
Two million stars above...*somewhere*
Too many miles to space
That is what I'm seeing, across the city view
This is our reason, for admiring what you do

The Painted Smile

The canvas stretched for painting, shading,
colours fading, beauty raging

Trickle and blend,
from beginning to end
A glimmer lost,
But seizing tops and tails in life.

They have it now... I saw them leaving
Colours fading, beauty bleeding

Fierce, mighty was the story
Laced with sequins, and so much glory
Skies aflame, and lights refrain
A sky on canvas
that glows, untame.

The hand outstretched, light a streaming
Winning kisses, but a sky... misleading.

Swiftly flying, affection grows
And where it ended, was wrapped in bows
And shone, like sequins... those opal pearls
My hand outstretched began to curl

Wrapped around the bows and rings
Mighty love and feathered wings

They have it now...
The skies and eyes
We also have it,
Those painted smiles

Some Kind Of Energy

With my own kind of energy, I acknowledge the day
Gather some moments in my own kind of way
With tiredness, I'm nestled in a confusion of time
I think back to old fables, and the taste of dried thyme

An energy from somewhere, has devoted itself,
to a new taste of freedom, serene and immense
I see illusions and in confusion...
I come close, I let go
And in your eyes, I reflect...
I ebb... and I flow

Pure hearts, finding reason... the need, and the must
Reading old fables, books laden with dust
I'm alive, enigmatic...
I dance in... then I go
And your heart, is my rhythm...
It will ebb... it will flow

I had some kind of feeling, I can barely recall
And in the distance, an image... to far to be sure
But the existence of some things,
we just may never know
And like the tales, and the fables...
We will all... ebb and flow

Mesmerising

The sky looks like the sea.
Rippling spirals, across the horizon, are mesmerising me.

The sea looks like the sky.
Frothy circles, above the tide
And horizontal patchy streaks, of charismatic light.

A sky that sways, as sea obeys.
A life that works as one.
Higher tide, and lower cloud
The wings of gulls, the grey white shroud.

What *calls* like the sky
and what *looks* like sea

are a million voices resting with thee
I can chase every mirage...
the luxury in life
I can look up and beyond
And awaken my mind
And through this very experience,
I can see them as free...
The sky and the sea

Take a look... look at thee

As It Rotates

Enigmatic is the Soul
It rotates within you, like a wheel, or a ball.
Silent is the Heart,
as it helps you to move closer...

to the Soul.

Together as one,
is the soul with the Heart
They evolve...
like a painting
And rotate...
like an art.

Problematic is the world,
like a dagger to the Soul
But you know the rhythm of your heart,
It will be rotating through it all.

Together, just together,
is the Soul within the Heart
They can, and will, evolve as one
For they may never be apart.

Enigmatic is the Soul
It rotates within *you*,
like a wheel, or a ball.

Silent is the Heart,
as it helps *you*...to move closer...to the Soul...

And to ourselves.

The Chiming

As the blood flows through your heart,
a river beckons, as it staggers towards to the edges,
and it beckons still
I wait to feel the velveteen
I wait for hearts to flow... enrapture me
And beckon me
I drift away, I'm swept away
So wakeful is my night
A broken sky breaks all the hearts
above the rivers edge
A beat is lost, until tomorrow and beneath the river bed

I hear the trickle, I taste the air, I know not of the den
I lie awake to drift and hear the beckoning farewell
I saw a dipper scooping water
Upon a stepping stone
Towards the edge of every river, I greet the new unknown
As the blood flows through your heart,
I walk towards... the beveled light
I think of blood flow... heart bestow...
I'm swept away tonight

There Was Space (part one)

We stretch the space around us and it's panoramic now
Shadows stretch and blow me kisses, and I felt them on my br

We could be taking photographs, or maybe even one!
As my earrings glisten in the light of a pixelated sun

Clouds resemble a mass of people,
with hands stretched out in prayer.
The self esteem of nature boasts of months that lie ahead

The space outstretched, has found itself!
It has waltzed all over town
More kisses carried by the breeze,
for there's no shelter to be found

Vastness, overwhelming... but it gives me space to gasp
I would like to go,
explore,
and *really gasp some more*

But it could take a while to find a path...
If I could find a path at all

There Was Space (part two)

More kisses blew my way, and I *felt* them... on my face
Like a multi coloured burst of words you spoke unto my face
But fantasy may climb and fall, like stardust on the castle wall
And outline every kiss you blow, towards my blushing face

In pixilated sun, a breeze and love collide,
Clouds resemble a mass of birds, with wings unto the light
My love for life is overwhelming, I would like to dwell some
more...
And swiftly choose a place to be... beyond the castle wall

And once again...more kisses, to embrace
A sky as white as bleached out linen, it wraps up the embrace
As if it were a spotlight surrounding where I am
And *I really gasp some more* as reciprocate...

...Embrace

Lighter Notes

Stories People Tell

I am yet another cat, that does not beside a broom
just waiting for my next ride to a night of doom and gloom
I will never bring you bad luck,
but I will never bring you good
I am just a black cat
Can we make that understood?

I sit upon the window ledge (I thought you'd like to know)
And I move along my territory, just strutting as I go!
I'm looking for a Queen, like all us Tom cats do
And I'd like the warmest cuddle, but maybe not from you

For that would all depend if you are out to label me
(Believe me, I'm loving cat...not a witchcraft mystery)
I'm not the witches 'familiar' with her potions and her spells
And my owner has no pointed hat...
Those are stories people tell

At home we have a saucepan, not a massive cauldron pot
So I am just a black cat
Do you agree with me or not?
I never did like labels, and my collar's in the way
But I am loved by both my owners
And that... I have to say

Thank you for your understanding
Now I'm out to look for love
As I'm just one of many black cats...
And we strut our funky stuff

Happy Times

I'm out and about,
looking for finds
Glass to upcycle,
the bubble bath kind.

The empty bottles,
where love was stored
The spray, and the cream,
that ladies explored.

The silky smoothness of body lotion
The pastel colours
in every potion
In and out of little shops
Finding bottles and bottle tops
Some with ribbons wrapped around
Clitter clatter, that glassy sound
A pleasant odour, of tea tree oil
Glass that bevels,
like crumpled foil.

Glassy miniatures of every type
Polka dots and happy times
Some are jars from marmalade
Those little things that glass has made
Overjoyed am I today,
shopping glassy,
the budget way.

Handwritten

Old and dated or mood elated?
What to write and how to seal
Flowing finely, neat and tidy
True blue ink, smear-free.
But will you be "Dear" or
is that out-dated?

And how to sign off...
tradition or not?
If I a mistake,
I'll be starting again.

Should I share my emotions?
And if so...when?
Ah, but no!
That's a bit cheeky
I feel I should be...
just a little more sneaky.

Writing flowing,
slightly leaning
A little untidy,
but with plenty of meaning
Hand written letters,
a love induced flow.

But what have I written?

...wouldn't you like to know!

Are You Alright Love?

We were in the bar
(as we often are)
And there was a bit of
push and shove
A guy came over,
tapped my shoulder
and asked...
"Are you alright love?"

I was trying to ignore him
but I had really had enough
Especially when asked me
if I liked a bit of rough.

I hit him with my handbag
It took him by surprise
I wouldn't recommend it
He could have blacked my eyes.

I called the bouncer over,
and what do you think he said?
He asked
"Are you alright love?"
Do you fancy going to bed?"

Free

Yippee!
I'm eighty three
My husband's dead
And I'm finally free.

I'm going on holiday
to sit by the pool
I'll wear a bikini
And behave like a fool.

In two months time,
I'll be eighty four.
Gonna buy a new toaster
and a laminate floor.

Eat chocolate biscuits,
and have time, just for me!
Yippee...
You know what?
I'm finally
free.

To Be A Cat

His Cat, purring it's life away into your lap
Sitting on the arm of a vintage chair...
not a care in the world, and I mean, not a care
Like "I was here first... and I made myself known
   Pawing, playing... in my *very own* home

The cat, so serious, The cat, always wise
The cat, such a smartass, but that's no surprise
   Purring, Such purring... then cleaning it's fur
A fine healthy coat, and another fine
Purrrrrrrrr...

The cat struts about in show-boating style
With fur slowly floating in the sunlight that shines
And so through the window
is where the cat takes the stage...
   A jump to the shelf
   where a book turns it's page
A bit of a clatter, but that doesn't matter
Fur falling, then floating, I see...
   The cat, as it leaps, and looks round the room,
And he will soon be, where planning to be

Knocks books off the shelf...
just to knock something else
But what the cat wants, he will certainly get...

Such purring, fur floating...
While the owner is noting...
It's time for a trip to the vet!

For The Diary

Some Things

I rarely write about the things I believe in,
   Or the love that I'm in -
   Or the mind from within
I rarely write about my country or home,
   Or the opinions of others -
   Or the spine that they've grown
I write about *things*
And I write from a wish,
as episodes of wisdom will not go amiss

I don't write to provoke
   Or to stand in your way -
   Or to gather my senses,
once they've chosen their way
I don't dwell on a past life,
   Or delve into yours -
   Or shout for an audience,
if I find I'm ignored
I write about *things*
Or I write for one thing
   One moment -
   Or reason -
That a someone may bring

Go Adrift

In our smile is the naked poignant heart,
bearing it's feelings, forever, and so far.
Remnants of beauty a million stars
A thousand emotions, all naked...
they are.

For the smiles and the splendor
And the feelings that pour...
Spill them out, let them gather on your lips...
they are more...
More than kind, more than pretty, and not easy to explain.
But they piece together puzzles,
In some mortal kind of way

There is far more to your lips,
than the smile.. you go adrift.
There are naked pure emotions,
that I cherish, that I kiss.

And in your most expressive way, you may alternate your style
I love and watch you go adrift,
And feel your naked smile.

The Three Minute Timer

I sit inside the hourglass,
waiting for the fall
The fall of sand, where every grain, will cover Polly's wall.

And I sit inside the throw and spin
where pebbles broken, shine
Then every grain will cover me,
and finally all is fine.

The hourglass had travelled far, wrapped up, in some old new
You stood it on the outside wall,
beside my ballet shoes.

I sat, curled up, with countless grains, a sifting through my
hands
I say "one minute, one minute left,
'til your wish is my command".

And then you lift me to the light,
inside this glass of time.
And all we feel,
are sandy grains
that swiftly fall,
with vibes and rhyme...

And just one second,
one second left...
of sifting sand, where we once met...
where every saint, held every hand.
On Kernow soil, our days were planned.

The Downpour

And now I just lose myself in the rain, *as it falls*
But I am told I'm just lost, on a land where *love calls*
The land where you will never see lovers by day
But at night, they'll be there,
and for the night, they will stay

And here, I can sway
from the street and the crowds
I will walk like a lady, and think out aloud
Take off my shoes, and curl up my toes,
and think back to his white shirt and black dickybow
His truest of words will be there *when love falls*
He'll be counting my footsteps, as the deep *rain will call*

As it falls, love calls,
when love falls, rain will call...

Saint Agnes

What a hilly climb
What a mist
And under my feet, a street,
that twists.
What a pretty dusk
What a night
And a clatter of the coral bright.

What a sailing boat
What a chime
On St. Agnes beaten climb.
What a day as passers-by,
may cast their eyes on sailors lives.

What a precious home, a glow
I see your plant pots out on show
While gulls will head for flight...
And the windmills spin delight,
around the pots so watered well...
To Agnes, I will go.

What a fragile urchin
What a pretty thing
On sandy castle beaches
Where the nights are drawing in.
What a village boasting shape
What a lantern to your face
Model homes of mini places
What a smile on me!

The corn is floating in the breeze
What a sea...of ivory.

Really, Always

Some things never *really* go away
Hand crafted dolls - A teapot on display
The soft and dusty butterfly was made from feathers
and a clip – and was placed onto the purple curtains,
often it would slip ---
Nothing lasts forever but do things ever *really* leave?
I kept seeing Herons on the Towy,
through binoculars, that I believe ---
were kept inside a dark brown leather case
This house was my escape ---
The sacred heart and well-worn books
The doorbell and the old brass hooks
Clothing draped in drafty places
and heat that filled the room
The view of Towy river, was my childhood
winding view ---
I would gaze at fifties tableware
Or the a blue and orange rug
Drink from stylish dated cups
(We never drank from mugs) ---
I traced my footsteps on the stairs
And always found *that something* there,
Like one brown monkey, soft and clean
waiting for his monkey dream
She travelled all those miles with me,
My nameless monkey, worn and cream
Fighter jets I swear I saw, on many early nights
Something rather scary about the battle-like of flights
It's just a plane, they'd say to me, and like the
dogs that roam outside, they'll come and go *as quick as that!*
And bid this house *goodnight*

But All I Am

I lay my eyes upon the day,
I don't complain
I think of what might have been,
who I've not yet seen
I don't complain

I close my eyes and turn away,
I'm in the rain
I feel the sun upon my hair
And people stare
But all I am... is in the rain

I lay my eyes upon the day,
I'm swept away, just swept away
I see an arrow in a tree,
Was it you... who set it free?
I close my eyes and turn away
I've felt the sun, I've felt the rain
I never knew what might have been
A love I met, but never seen

I lay myself upon the bed
Words are turning, in my head
Will I ever set them free?
I close my eyes... in need of sleep
And as I do, the words I feel...
are soon to be, more real to me
I'm swept away, I'm swept away
I lay my eyes upon the day
But that was then...
that was today

And So It Was

It was the strangest land, and the most buoyant sea,
below open clouds, that cradled me.
And it was the buoyant sea, so adrift with time,
that wave by wave, helped me to shine.

I'd been awake for hours, on the strangest land
The flames of rays, had scorched my hands
Below open clouds, and on muddy sand,
I had the strangest feelings, on the strangest land

With beauty, with aroma, and her foam to bathe
To the sea I will be, one timeless slave
But I'd been awake for hours, so I thought of sleep
Thought to gaze at the clouds, over land, as they creep
And across my palms, came the wettest waves
And it occurred to me, that I'd been asleep for days

So I had not been awake, not seen the light of each day
I had been captured by clouds, and cradled by waves...
Been led to believe, that I so needed sleep.
On the strangest of land, where the sea foam would seep

The Sail Away

A Rose by name, A surface for you soul
A thorn, the shape of a sail
in the rock pool by the bay
A Rose by name, You are striking for sure
A Velveteen curl -
Nothing less, nothing more

A thorn to your mind, A sail by shape
You sail in the breeze, to the cove – you escape
See my Rose touch the edge of the rocks, of the pool
where I made my pledge, to be a fool –
a fool to the cove and all that it knew -
and what it meant, to those who hid,
those who smuggled as smugglers did

I want to be the Rose – And want you to be the sail
Let us both climb aboard –
Let us go – sail away!
I am hiding every thorn – And I've a thorn to my mind
But we'll sail away in velvet cloaks –
For it's the breeze that we will find

The Fading Light

You are the dark desire above all those lights
And your mood will change, as always, tonight
You bring yourself to the streets, and onwards to me
And I wait amidst the sky, of a playful kind of glee

I can see you there, in the black that you wear
And come the night, you will take both my hands
Around architecture bold,
and rich...
we wander
we see the city perform a kiss...

but from where?

You are the fading of the light
You are the one...
the city Knight
My blackened heart will see us both, as we blend
As we walk barefoot, I live for the knight...
Under lights where no lover could pretend

I found all of your darkness... above all of the lights
Diversely gentle, you are the essence
...of the meaning
...of the night
You take silver from armour, you were more ...
...and still are
And through my voice as it whispers...
You are the knight... from afar

The Hidden Meanings

Was I Ever Born?

I wasn't born under a rhyming planet, or somewhere *between*
the slate and granite
But somewhere *under* a chaotic sky,
my voice would travel, it was dignified

From *inside* a shell, with my elbowed crawl,
I saw the *outside*,
and shared a smile with it all
I felt someone nudge me, above where I lay,
above other planets on a land of red clay

A vibration, a shudder, I felt on my skin, like a rhyme
for no reason, it seeped deep within
I lay out on the granite, I drew on the slate,
My dignified whisper awaited my fate

I was never born under a rhyming planet
That's if I was ever born at all
But I vaguely remember a beveled ground
There's a chance I was washed up on the shore...

...and found lying there asleep, in a storm

Now under the granite sky am I, and buoyant with the tide
And *below* the essence of the chaos, that releases all its pride

The Fern

They are timeless, And today I see a few
Just a few of many, that gather here,
for you
Rarely are they spoken of, but always they will be,
the symbol of you...for life
A memory,
for me

So they are prehistoric, In darkest forest shades
You will see them, always , And I relive the stories made

The toughness of the detail
The resilience of the Fern
And the wondering of you... stood here and there...
talking of its worth

A Fern for life, within the garden tucked away, it stands
And deep within the forest walk, touched by youthful hands
The green, the feel, the counting of the leaves
The wary fox that watches us, And the fern...
Where are it's seeds?

A Fern will always thrive for you, And grow on higher ground
I will see it sewn, within my mind... long after you have gone

Of The Time

You climb onto the clock of all time and you break away from
your mold
You often walk where the clothing is draped, over the back of
chair...
with it's creases and folds.

You climb onto the clock of all time, and it took you so many
years
Often you would walk past the windows and doors, of the sho
with their stairs and their tiers

Now you're wearing those dresses that go back in time
Sometimes with bling, and an eyeliner fine
You strut as you walk, in private it seems
With lace and silk ribbons, made
only for dreams.

Now wearing those dresses, you know what you like
You know who you are...At last, you saw light!
The climb to the top, to the tip of the time, and you winked as
you got there,
and you made a man smile.

You're out there for sure, and time is your own
You admire the thoughts, of him in your home
And in one favourite dress, you climb onto he clock
And he stands below you...
saying "hey love, you rock!"

In The Garden

Pulling up weeds, such softness and scent, I am always about on
the lawn
With dirt on my jeans, all torn at the seams, I may not look like a
lady at all
I sure know a fairy and her family too.
They like taking pictures of a trowel or two
They own water pistols
which they keep in my pots
Have a point n' shoot camera,
for their days at the croft
May they dance with the summer,
and sleep with the light
May they sing with the autumn,
or ride on the flight...
of those migrating birds,
as they swallow and swift
Above slow growing grass
and those fairies that split...
their days between wickedness upon the new lawn
And the days that they sneak to my house, for it's warmth

The Maiden At Sea

Burying my thoughts between the grains of silver sequin sand
Looking ahead, I see a maiden in the name of the swaying lan
Draped in jewels, the sea is her,
and she rises to your hair
Her charm is floating, harmonising,
threads of seaweed bare
So elegant, a maiden swoons
She is the sleeping sea
She gathers trinkets, broken shells
And silver sand she spills for free
I hear her spaceous calls and thrills, and sequin-chiming bells
And dancing waves alongside caves, is where the Maiden dwe

The Red Kite

Be up there, like a kite in a transparent sky
Soar with it all, at a height
Leave yourself free to be captured by a breeze
 as it pulls on the strings of a cautious flight
It will navigate - your every emotion
They will rattle in the air – a transparent sky
A wingspan stretched to it's full extent
Waiting – for what could be – in it's sight

Be up there, like the kite on it's way
that knows every limit, elusive the prey
Over the valleys, silent it's flight
Pulling on heartstrings, the width of the kite
The wind through the wings - will now battle - then sway
The make-believe raptor, the height of the day
And the steady perfection of the skill of the Kite
Over the valleys – on with the flight

Distant Miles

Silver falls and trails the table, how green your life may be
Boho rugs under the table, and secrets calling me
Silver falls and takes the water, how fine your life may be
Conkers in a woven basket, and chicken soup for tea

Marble falls a twist of colour, water fresh but cold
Walking boots and coloured scarves, a venture getting old
Marble falls, a name to me, a mystery now cold
Rocks to gather... carry home, then treat, and shine the bold

Silver marbles, metal-made, and heavy in the jar
I kept them as they were a gift, I've no idea where they are
Silver marbles for the boys, just honey for a jar
I'm flying through my memories, but I never travel far

Boho falls upon my table, drapes it's little lines,
And walking boots outside the door, for all those distant mile
Conkers, rocks and aching shoulders, a face of weathered lin
Getting older, but shining bolder, thanks for all those times

What We Borrow

A night so beautiful,
with no thoughts of tomorrow
A naked wisp, you have aimed to follow
A solar sky chasing the clouds
Where a million words are spoken aloud
The night so young, with thoughts of today
And an angelfish floating, before swimming away
Naked the moon, like a lens to the wisp
Be steady and waiting for the moon to eclipse.
A night as it blooms, has no care for tomorrow, we just spend
our time with the moments we borrow.
Tonight we have forecast the sky over sea, will be cloudless and
ready, to be touched, to be seen
And a line of thin light, like a road to your heart, will beat
beautiful rhythms, as the night will depart
Naked the moon, and shying away
is the exotic and merciful break of the day.

It Didn't Exist

I have made it so high, above every bramble,
and to the sun,
as it shines

This is the place... Sun to the heat
but there will never be a burn to your skin
Brambles unkempt, will twist as they curl,
but they have never attempted to sting

And this place, a tree for a home
A rope-handled swing over weeds as they roam
I am here for a lifetime, I've been rescued from me
This is the place...
I so chose to be

And I know this place... like the back of my hand
The grass here, it dances, at the sun in command
I am here for a lifetime
I stroll and I swing
This is the place, where our loved ones can sing

But this is the place, that doesn't exist,
It just kept coming back, like the sun through the mist

This place that I saw, was all in my mind
And even my dreams... are unable to find
The sun to the heat
the sun through the mist
And all I escaped from...

That didn't exist

In The Red

It looked innocent, so fragile, so deep it was in red
A piece of tissue paper, like crepe, in deepest red
Slight, the curl of every edge,
torn, opaque and shy
Like a petal that had been abandoned, deep in the reddest dye

I looked at it's fragility, as it fell from its own blood
Torn apart, the paper, deep in the red I love
Curling in its innocence, the beauty that it was
It needed to be handled, with the care it had just lost

My petal sign, a deepest warmth, without a flower bed
Should I place you on the roadside, in memory the dead?
Red so fragile, red like blood
A petal spiked with dye
In the red, a flowerbed abandoned you...
but why?

Just Round The Corner

The Other Day

Another day is lurking - and there's a lyric in your soul
And in the crevice - flowers take a glance at the unknown
They look up and over many petals while confined to their ow
space -
And I guess they wonder why Buttercups are under every fac

Another day is slipping into the crumbling of dusk
It seems to be that devils watch the weeds, like Buttercups
Watching youngsters holding them - underneath their chin-
Just one of life's memories - like the lyric you shall sing...

Well this *other day* is smiling - and in the crevice you will clim
If you want a taste of the unknown - or a rhythm to a line
I looked it up - the Buttercup!
And I found it sleeping small
Tucked up tightly for the night - but for the devils beck and ca
In every yellow dream they have - or in every night-time call
The Buttercups announce their presence – *"we're available t.*
dawn"
And after that - another day will come knocking on your door
Sing your lyrics - be a dreamer - be a devil for a song
And look towards the Buttercup – this *other day* is born

Under The Pier.

There is divinity and humanity
under the pier and the view
There is no-one to bow down to
but I bow unto the moon

There is beauty and infinity
under the willow lake so pale
And every tie of elegance,
will touch the swan that sails

There is eternity and tranquility
I can feel it in my wish
And all I see is golden dust,
and the tremor of your kiss.

There is diversity and energy
for those who understand
We took every day as ours,
and left them in our hands

To the pier and the moon I go
For here we walked away.
I left the garland of the willow,
I let it float upon the lake.

There is honestly and certainty
where the willow framed the view
I had so much to say back then, but I had so much to do.

The pier and the subtly
of the moon above the kiss
Fantasy, reality,
what a speechless, drifting wish.

We No Longer Roam

We bound twigs together with colourful rope
They were left on the bed of the woods
And scattered upon the fungi and debri
Twigs as unique as the woods

As we bound them together, the smell of sweet musk
Arose from the shavings, a mingled with green
Were they once a perch, for the small woodland birds?
Or were they catapults for the children we see?

Back to our youth, we understood who we were...
Together, we could climb, we could swing
And lift up your friends, and spin them round...
Did we forget who we were...
and everything?

Special moments, gathered twigs
And wrapping 'em up tight, in the woods
For they smelt so earthy, as earthy as they were...
In the gaps of the light... In the woods

Rarely did we see, any sunlight in there...
Deep...
within the density,
of life.
Where a thousand twigs, lay old and bare
and words had been carved with a knife

Carved out by lovers,
or names of the kids who entered the woods with their blade
Ribbons, from strangers who stretched up to tie them...
if I remember right... those were the days.

Cupids Arrow

Souls talking as they do,
within the centre of the night,
under a yellow sky of blue,
they change as they excite.
The breeze on both our faces, cleansing as they are.
Invigorating feelings, two Souls unaware.

The episode has come alive, the gleaming of the eyes.
Two Souls sing, they share their love, like sashays to the light.
Under a yellow sky of blue,
we hide between the covers.
And Cupid's arrow comes tonight,
and turns us into lovers
Two Souls making history,
on the inside they are bound.
Within the centre of the earth,
the lotus Souls were found.

The Unsung Dance

Life is asking us to spend more of our time dancing
a slow, slow dance
Where music is barely, barely audible, and we are enchanted,
by some kind of romance

Slowly dancing in the open hallway, tactile and smooth
Fingertips resting, and feeling each move
Skin barely touching... Just her... loving you.

Life is asking us to feel the flow through your spine
with the undisturbed music that mirrors your mind.
Slowly dancing in the space of your home
Two souls thriving... and neither are alone.

Background music, sensing rhythm...
Two souls touching, with two hearts singing
Music repeating... because life... is asking...

For the slowness of an unsung dance.

Sto Bene

Shooting stars, shadow hovering

Tantalise the sky

Overwhelmed with pleasure, am I

Beneath the trickling colour I see

Endless clouds, they glide with me

North above my tender eyes

Every star doth tantalise

(**Sto Bene** – meaning – **I'm Fine**
In the Italian language)

Dead Of The Night

The moments wander,
and I'm left wondering... how they manage to leave so fast
For it's those little moments wandering... that leave us in the
dark

I wonder why my heart keeps pounding, in the dead of every
night
Or thoughts I cannot piece together, are nonsense in the light

I wonder why I ever wandered...
It's human nature, so they say
And did I chose the dead of night, or did it just end up that w

Should I choose to be enlightened?
Should I search for some excitement?
Separate my pounding heart, while stories wait in lucid dark?

Enlighten me! I await my turn
See the sunlight, fail to burn
Excite me! I am strong today
I can wander... miles away

I can wonder... all I like
And shall not fear the dead of night...
my pounding heart or nonsense thoughts.
It's human nature, so I'm taught

Broken Fences

I love the rawness of your life, it speaks in many words -
Upon the wounded walks of life,
Upon this broken earth
I love the quirky broken fences, the worn and weathered look
The rustic aging beauty, found in shabby splintered wood

Such things in life may go unnoticed, or we frown at what we see
Like rusty nails we dare not touch... but that's *not* how I feel
With all the posts that lean and fall,
And with the moments that we steal -
We see the living dying grass, and we *know* that life is real
The twisting lives, like ragged clothes --
Or broken wounded hearts
The earth itself, robust but sad --
But we never look this far

I love the rawness of your life -
you know the ways to talk
And you too, love all those broken fences -
Upon wounded earth,
We've walked

This Heart Of Mine

She has touched his heart, he touched her soul
They entwine as one, as love doth grow
As souls will find, as hearts will pound...
the mind denies,
what love hath found

He has danced with joy, She has sung full bloom
as prisms curl across the room
Where music taught and smoothly plays
entwine like ringlets,
upon a stage

She has softened his heart He is healing her soul
as lovers define what all lovers know
As souls will rise and make-believe
as prisms curl before they leave

Lovers entwine, like music sheets
as notes and bars decide to meet
As dancers do as you define...
A voice will touch...
this heart of mine

Living In Hope

I live **in** the *one day...*
I will, and I may
I can but dream, I can dream life away

I live **on** the *one day...*
Like the story, I'd say
On the morn and the noon, and I'd give me away

I can live **with** the *one day...*
as always I say
I can sense every moment, I can sure live this way

I live **like** the *one day...*
Keeping feelings at bay
In the hope I can release...
watch them fly...

Then I'd **become** the *one day*

For The Soul

Hummingbirds

They hover over life, so often with a song
A magical supremacy, and life ticks on

...and on

One hundred flaps per second...
The successful beating wings
A captivating theory, as life ticks on

...and sings

And I take in the magnitude
of what they have achieved
It need not go unnoticed, if you can just believe

...believe

As life ticks on, so sings the bird
that hovers over life
And we sit under the summer rays,
of endless space and light
I contemplate, I dare to speak
I watch the Hummingbird
And life ticks on... *and on...*
and sings...
And I *believe* it's every word

Letting It Happen

She can't let him go -
He has a place in her soul

As do the leaves to the tree -
And the waves to the sea

And he wants her to stay -
Hear the leaves as they sway

And take to the seas -
To be kissed by her breeze

Two souls become one
And together they glide -

Through the leaves on the trees -
And the strength of the tide

No Tomorrow

You should shine like the sun, glow like the moon,
Love as if there is no tomorrow,
And for whom?

...For yourself

...And the people
You can shine on,
with the moon you're looking for

If there is to be no morn tomorrow
You will be safe, so safe to know,
that you have shared yourself
...with someone

...And you helped that someone glow

So like the sun, you rise and set

Like the moon, you wax and wane

In my heart, you are the solitude
...And here

...You will remain

Shadow Angle (part one)

I walk with my shadow
She leads and I follow

She stretches beyond, and my eyes abide
And if I am needing to keep an eye on the time –

I just look at my shadow - the giveaway sign

She'll be waiting for sunlight and the right time of day
Then she will catch me completely -
She is so smart in this way
She'll grab my attention, she'll step right ahead
And over the verges my shadow is lead,
by me on my own – I am on my way home –
on a warm summer eve, and I pull up my sleeves
I daydream of many a shadow I've cast
She's a place near me, she's a piece of my heart

I feel slightly sad when I'm alone at the door
As this is the time, when I'm *needing* her more
For without her, my shadow,
I am lost and exposed –
I'm in my own world, and I follow my clone

Shadow Angle (part two)

I'm facing the sun - early afternoon,
an autumnal feel - I'm facing the sun
My leader will prompt me – she hides in the grass
Follows me walking to the cold underpass
She's noble, precise, she rises then hides –
Her dark cooper outline, is soothing my eyes

She is my leader - I follow her ways
Although she's behind me - and I look both ways
She stands on the edge of the underpass wall –
Touches graffiti - and makes sense of it all
She shivers and reaches for the nourishing light
Lies out on the grass - in copper delight

I'm facing the sun – late afternoon
Dusk is my shadow – She loses the sun
My leader will tell me to follow the one –
As bold as the copper – for the day is now done
So I go it alone
I run through the park
Dusk is my shadow, asleep in her dark

The Definition

The skyline defines us
It shapes us, and knows us
You sit on the sand, drawing lines with your hand...

Random the rocks, that lie close together
Slipping away in the strength of the weather
An easterly wind blows for the scene
And removes all the cobwebs from your mind and your dream

Random the rocks, that lie close together
Breathless the walkers, fierce the weather
Rocks oval smooth... so vocal they crackle,
under your shoes, as you walk through the battle
In tune with the wind,
is the howl to your hearing
Clouds in a race, with blue sky appearing

No shelter around, so put on your gloves
Pull tight your jacket...
and don't lose your love...
for this raging of beauties we seek when we're here
for the rocks as they stumble...
under cloud, under clear...
under shoes worn by walkers, who in tune with the sky
will sway through the battle, where the gulls soar and cry

Driftwood a creaking,
sea calmly flowing
A jingle of shells,
and the north wind a blowing
A totem pole standing
And we pull the sand in...
we want our toes to be covered,
where the north wind a blows

The skyline defines us
It shapes us, and knows us
You sit on the sand,
drawing lines with your hand...

A breeze leaves us trembling
on a day worth remembering
A sound softly speaking,
by the driftwood a creaking
Is the jungle of shells...
on the night they are greeting
And we gather our senses,
into warm hearts a beating

On The Mural

I vowed to see you in my sleep
You are precious,
like the mural on the wall
The one I take a closer look at,
so I may be inside a mood so deep...
or a world so small

I was there to see the foxes peep...
Just like the one's upon the wall...
that roam the roads of stitching steep...
for they inspire one and all

Shall we help them now before we sleep?
Shall we find a mood so deep?
And maybe take a closer look
at the hills where foxes peep?

I love the mural facing me,
and the strength of every thread
And I vow to see you in my sleep,
within my slumber deep...
and within a dream...
within my head

I vowed to care for foxes sleep
They are as precious as the mural on the wall
They are the ones I look out for,
And they help me... to be safe inside a world so small...
Or a mood so deep
Deep enough to bring on my sleep

A Fine Glance

Grey skies above a Butterfly dancing -
A Grasshopper resting - under grey skies above

A Tree creeper climbing –
a murmur is rhyming
A Dove is close by -
and the wishing well sings

Throw in some pennies and make you a wish
And whatever you wish for, will see you in bliss

And under a grey sky, we hear from above
A Dunnock exchanging her peace with a Dove

Grey skies surround us,
like pebbles in dust, lie heavy above us
and beneath where we trust...
Our parting with pennies, shall invite us to dance
And rest under grey skies
And take a fine glance...
As nature is climbing and rhyming by chance

Thoughts Out

 A lifetime of being unable to shout about anything
Suppressed and confined to her thoughts
and maybe – everything

*"Head for the woods - stumble barefoot
The wild is uneventful today"*

Something was calling her fragmented mind -
"The wild is uneventful today"

She stumbled barefoot, fell to her knees –
in the sounds, in the woods
Now **she** spoke the words
*"I'm here on my knees, I came here to breathe
Where the demons are lost -
And where the believers believe"*

No one responded to her fragmented mind
Nothing was needed, just the light of her eyes
Bare hands on earth, and bare exposed knees
Rhythmical chatters from the crow and the trees

Inhale – exhale –
Breathe to oneself
Fearless the sounds, and there was something else –
Now **she** spoke once more
*"No longer suppressed –
No longer confined –
I give my life to the woods,
and my soundest
sound mind"*

Deeper Notes

Modernity

They are here, just here above me,
so wild behind the scenes
And oh so full of antics...
a bit like my old dreams

But I've been doing well down here,
ignoring them each night
The wild and wicked phase they go through,
that *they* call, *living life*

They *are* the painting in the gallery,
modernity, I'd say!
But I left the antics of these people,
so that I could change my ways

And so they tempt me, with the frivolity
and they call me to join in
They follow me to every room,
hoping I'll give in
But I plan to leave them carry on,
let them flaunt above my day!
They follow me upstairs, downstairs...
But I have changed my ways
I feel they are about to call me,
with a knock upon my door
But I have strength and certainty

I want so much, so much more...
than the wildness of parties, and the egotistic phase
Modernity, I'd say,
has now seen better days

Anatomical

I can't fix what is broken, how would it ever be the same?
He's previous, I dust him almost every day
With sentimental charm, he is the character I love
Today he's sitting next to me, looking relatively robust

But I think he's had his time with me, his form is looking aged
He's barely upright on the shelf, so I lie him on my page
Wooden smooth, he has his place, next to a bedside light
He is the *something* I will miss so much,
he taught me how to look at life

Damn...I wish he could be fixed
But would he ever be the same?
Sometimes we have to say goodbye, and learn from all we gained
He's been the figure for an artist, a figure for my shelf
And one thing I am certain of, is that he can't be *something* else

Merging

We will merge as one, like two tears
We have wept those tears, like two grievers
We understand loss

... And like two believers of the same sadness,

... we merge as **one**

Both tears linger, they gaze as one
They fall upon tomorrow's sun
They shall not scream, nor will they hide

They are **one** sadness

...And as **one**, they cried

The Final One

You are alone in your beauty, the final tear
You just need to let go, so you may disappear
...become absorbed by the soil, or dried by the heat,
on the industrial vastness, the tarmac on the street

There will be no more
You *are* the final one
You came with the rain, but will leave with the sun
You cling to each other before falling away,
into the soil, or onto the grey

There are no others
And I shall now never hear
...another sweet raindrop, or a delicate tear
But I think I may catch you, and have you here on my skin

I feel you nourish my senses,
like the earth you lie within

The Blue Room

A soulful of strumming in a light filled room,
where dinosaurs stand above a border of blue

The soulful sound that echoes in time,
down a sunlit staircase,
where it's entirety
shines

Notice the strumming, in rhythm it calls
As gentle
and restful,
as the night time that falls

One young boy,
found his love in strings
A guitar, like his heartbeat,
as the bluest voice sings

Images of space, and plectrums in jars
A desert for dinosaurs, space travels far
The happiest **blue** that has stayed with his soul
It echoes throughout to the journey unknown

It's Getting Late

Under the archway of bricks and broken stone
Company, I'm craving -
Although I came to be alone
I'm cold, and getting colder, I try to focus on the shapes
Of broken bricks and paving stones -
through the hours getting late

Illusions crawling in the cold, that jog my memory
The company I'm craving for, is sat right next to me?
I tread upon a paving stone, it rattles like a snake
I watch the stones move under me -
I hear the echoes that they make

Under the archway of bricks and broken stone
I chose to be here, and for an hour
I chose to be alone

Old and getting older, is today, that cannot stay
And I hear it echo as it travels –

And as it *hears me* -
walk away

Hand In Hand

The Quiet

If you're passing this way,
come find me
I am with the songbirds,
should you want me to sing

If you're tired of your journey, come find me
And I will hold you
for the love we are in

You will know who I am,
when you discover the quiet--
the hidden,
mysterious
heart

The quiet, the whisper
The luminous skies
The songbird a singing
The love undenied

You will hear all of this,
through the beat of a heart,
that will be here--
til death do us part

The Tumbledown

I see my beloved standing behind the fountain
And smiling through the water of this town
The highs and lows of every rainfall,
the sloping
tumbledown

My beloved walks towards me, and holds me in his arms
Lifting me, onto his shoulders
I feel no older than I am

The place where I, first found this man, was on the other side of
town
And on that day I saw him, through the rain
that tumbled down

This most beloved fountain, with its rumbling of tears
And the beloved falling of the rain, that we never fail to hear

And my beloved... So beloved, who holds me close today
is here to read my poetry, about the fountain in the rain
The highs and lows of every rainfall, and of every frame of mind
Of each and every season coming, and the life we can't rewind

The Escape

Dampened air is evaporating over the rocky road
The universe, (not yet discovered) reaches out and screams
It's been mumbling - I've heard it speaking -
between the waking trees

And all this morn has seen

Shoppers chores and screeching doors, my ears feel the pain
Like a rumbling of the universe -
Noise to drench the town - like rain

There's one escape that shimmers -
on the left of the rocky road
Weeds can drown so peacefully in a river - free of screams
I shall leave the town get on with things,
and surround myself with dreams

And all these morning scenes

Dampened air, a castaway, has long gone to the sky
And the town (not yet discovered) can yell with every step
And while it does - I shall be sitting here -
holding back the day - holding back the universe -

What will morning bring my way?

There In Our Minds

A web of memories, *hang* in my mind
Irregular shapes *sweep* through my mind --
And those choices we make,
that *drift on* in our minds --
may stay there, as lessons in life

A map of those journeys, they *move* in my mind
Trodden away like the *dust* of my mind
Ground that we walked on
so many times --
when too tired to sleep --
or too exhausted, our minds
We have strolled the shapes,
and woven through webs --
And through all the life cycles,
with each step we tread --
we are all missing *something* we have so longed to find
And all missing *someone* who is *there* in our minds

Got To Love An Umbrella

Pitter Patter, one for sorrow
My umbrella, but yours to borrow
Pitter patter, take my jacket...
but look after it, for it cost a packet
Pitter patter, bring it on
Thursday coming, Tuesday gone
One for sorrow, Wednesday wet
Under cover, and no regret
With the rain, a timid shatter
on *my* umbrella... pitter patter

I've made mistakes, in years gone by...
Some send shivers down my spine
I saw one for sorrow, but let it go
Just like today, this Wednesday woe
So pitter patter, river deep,
brighter days and beauty sleep
My umbrella, but *yours* for now
Feel the rainfall on my brow

Pitter patter, gentle fall
Bags of chips, wrapped up and warm
But hush... I do not hear...
the Pitter patter...
on my umbrella

A weird thing...
this Wednesday weather

Thank You For Reading

Biography:

I was born in South Wales in 1967.
My family background has mixed heritage, and within this,
I mostly feel that I identify with Wales (Cymru)
and Italy (Italia)
I spent a lot of time, and have a lot of,
wonderful childhood memories of
both the West of Wales and Cornwall (Kernow)
I'm also a spare time artist who admires art in general.
I have always been a quiet person,
and more interested in natural environments
than in city life, and maybe that is because I am quiet.
It enables me to think and feel at ease in such a chaotic world.
But who knows!
All I know is that poetry has helped me find myself
almost fully. And I say *almost*, because I'm not sure
we ever stop finding ourselves in one way or another.
Together with my writing,
my passion for music, art, wildlife,
and poetry in general, I'm more able to understand,
and accept, who I truly am.

Printed in Great Britain
by Amazon

70797603R00061